Tall Grass

by

Brian Harris

FOUNDED 1830

NEW YORK HOLLYWOOD LONDON TORONTO

SAMUELFRENCH.COM

ISBN 978-0-573-66245-4   Printed in U.S.A.   #22312

IMPORTANT BILLING AND CREDIT
REQUIREMENTS

THE BECKETT THEATRE at THEATRE ROW

ROGER ALAN GINDI in association with NUTMEG PRODUCTIONS LLC
presents

TALL GRASS

A New Dark Comedy by
BRIAN HARRIS

with

MARK H. DOLD   **EDWARD O'BLENIS**   **MARLA SCHAFFEL**

Set Design
CAMERON ANDERSON

Costume Design
GAIL BALDONI

Lighting Design
JOSH EPSTEIN

Sound Design
SHARATH PATEL

Fight Director
RICK SORDELET

Production Manager
ADURO PRODUCTIONS

Production Stage Manager
SARAH BIERENBAUM

Assistant Stage Manager
ADAM GROSSWIRTH

Marketing
HHC MARKETING

Press Representative
KEITH SHERMAN & ASSOCIATES

General Manager
GINDI THEATRICAL MANAGEMENT

Company Manager
A. SCOTT FALK

Casting
JUDY HENDERSON

Directed by
NICK CORLEY

"THE BUSINESS PROPOSAL"

Scene 1: A restaurant

Scene 2: An office

Scene 3: A restaurant

Paula LaBrek .... MARLA SCHAFFEL

Trevor Palumbo .... MARK H. DOLD

Waiter .... EDWARD O'BLENIS

"THE GERBIL"

Place: A dining room

James .... MARK H. DOLD

Dog .... EDWARD O'BLENIS

Margaret .... MARLA SCHAFFEL

"TALL GRASS"

Place: A living room

Chester .... EDWARD O'BLENIS

Dottie .... MARLA SCHAFFEL

Howard .... MARK H. DOLD

UNDERSTUDIES

Understudies never substitute for listed players unless a specific
announcement for the appearance is made at the time of the performance.

Understudy for *Waiter, Dog, Chester:* JORDAN MAHOME;

for *Paula, Margaret, Dottie:* AMY MALLOY; for *Trevor, James, Howard:* JIM PRICE.

THIS PRODUCTION WILL BE PERFORMED WITHOUT AN INTERMISSION.

THE BUSINESS PROPOSAL

CHARACTERS

PAULA LABREK   Late 20's
TREVOR PALUMBO Late 20's
WAITER

SCENES

Scene 1   A Restaurant Table
Scene 2   An Office
Scene 3   A Restaurant Table

TIME

The present.

Scene 1

(Curtain opens on **PAULA LABREK** *and* **TREVOR PALUMBO**, *both late 20's, seated in a corner of a dimly lit restaurant. Only their candle-lit table need be visible, next to a window.)*

PAULA. Imbeciles! That's who's running purchasing. Do you think they could ever pick a budget and stick to it? No it's always bottleneck this, lost shipment that.

TREVOR. You've lost shipments?

PAULA. Entire shipments, straight to the Bermuda Triangle for all I know. We should just fire purchasing – the whole damn department. Hire some housewives at Target. They buy things. They know how to meet a budget.

TREVOR. We automated purchasing a year ago. I heard that helped.

PAULA. That's because you work for a *smart* company. It's no wonder we have a 15-point share gap to you guys.

TREVOR. Share gaps come and go.

PAULA. I think Finance –

TREVOR. May I ask, how did you like the cod?

PAULA. The cod? Fine. Very codlike. And the lemon sauce was very lemony. How was your steak?

TREVOR. Good. Very meaty. The food was also good the last time we were here. Remember?

PAULA. Was that before or after the Taydon Borochek merger?

TREVOR. This was the first place I ever took you.

PAULA. Yes! We were switching the budget model over to Excel 11.0 – remember all the links broke down and I had to rush back to fix them?

TREVOR. I remember. Can you believe it's been two years?

PAULA. Tell me. Who would have guessed I'd still be stuck doing spreadsheets all this time?

TREVOR. I was referencing our relationship.

PAULA. Oh, yes, two years.

TREVOR. That's long enough to get to know someone pretty well, wouldn't you say? Do you feel you know me pretty well by now?

PAULA. Yes, I think so. Do you think you know me?

TREVOR. Paula, of course I know you.

> *(beat)*

I know that you're kind, and I know that you're beautiful –

PAULA. There's something I've been meaning to tell you.

TREVOR. Oh?

PAULA. It's about work.

TREVOR. Paula, do you see this?

> *(points to candle)*

PAULA. Yes?

TREVOR. This is a candle. Office environments don't normally have these.

PAULA. OK, fine.

TREVOR. No, go ahead.

PAULA. No, it's really not that important. Please go on.

TREVOR. Are you sure?

PAULA. Please.

TREVOR. All right. Did I mention that you're kind-hearted and beautiful?

PAULA. Yes, but don't worry, you're not boring *me*.

TREVOR. And that you care about me?

PAULA. Yes, you know that.

TREVOR. And that we've been going out now for two years.

> *(**PAULA** nods.)*

And you know that I love –

*(An annoying buzzing noise goes off and begins re-
peating.*

PAULA *whips out a Blackberry device and begins to type
furiously)*

Sorry. Stupid Blackberry.

(continues typing)

TREVOR. It's 10:00 Friday night.

PAULA. But only 7:00 on the West Coast.

TREVOR. Does that run your life? That Shackleberry! Can't
you just let go for once?

PAULA. That's easy for you. You never had to hold onto anything in your life.

TREVOR. That's not exactly fair.

PAULA. *(finishes typing)* Finished! Here, I'm turning it off.

(returns Blackberry to her purse)

Happy?

TREVOR. Can we, can both of us, just try to relax, for
once?

PAULA. No! All right, but only as an experiment.

TREVOR. Paula …

*(reaches for her hand and they share a moment. Then
the Blackberry goes off again.)*

PAULA. Damn.

*(pulls out Blackberry, frowns slightly, then fiddles with
it)*

Here now it's really turned off.

(returns it to purse)

TREVOR. Maybe you should answer it.

PAULA. No, we're supposed to be having a romantic
dinner

TREVOR. Look, Paula, you know that I think you're kind
hearted and beautiful and that you care about me and
that I love you. Even with your peculiarities. What I'm

trying to say is –

WAITER. *(entering)* And how is everything here?

PAULA. Oh, fine thanks.

WAITER. Excellent! And how did you like the cod?

PAULA. Delicious. Not too dry and the sauce was captivating. Did I detect a touch of tamarind with the lemon?

WAITER. Yes, excellent! And you sir, how did you find your steak?

TREVOR. Chatty yet truculent. No, fine. Everything was great.

WAITER. *(clearing table)* Excellent. Excellent. And have we left some room for dessert? We have chocolate and boysenberry soufflé, a raspberry truffle cake, peach and green tea ice cream?

PAULA. Just a coffee for me. Actually do you have espresso?

WAITER. Of course.

PAULA. Double espresso please.

WAITER. Excellent. And for you sir?

TREVOR. A decaf with some Baileys. Thanks.

WAITER. That's excellent. Just give me a moment.

(leaves with cleared dishes)

PAULA. That's the same "excellent" waiter we had two years ago.

TREVOR. I think I was about to ask you something.

PAULA. Can it wait a moment? I have to use the restroom. Okay?

TREVOR. Sure.

PAULA. Be right back!

(exits)

*(**TREVOR** stares ahead, watching her leave, then reaches into his pocket and glances down briefly, returning the object to his pocket. As he reaches again into his pocket, **PAULA** returns, causing him to return it to his pocket. She takes her purse and leaves again.)*

(TREVOR is briefly still, but then starts rearranging items on the table so that everything is symmetrical. He then takes a small square box out of his pocket and places it on the table in front of her chair. He fiddles a little bit more with it, making sure it's properly centered.)

WAITER. *(entering with coffees)* Here we are.

(beat)

Is that what I think it is?

TREVOR. Possibly.

WAITER. Excellent – I mean congratulations! Is that what you're supposed to say? And to the woman, I think it's "I'm so happy for you!"

TREVOR. You might be premature.

WAITER. Oh.

(looking in direction of restroom)

In the restroom?

(TREVOR nods.)

How long?

TREVOR. How long? I don't know, maybe about 30 seconds.

WAITER. Excellent! There's still time to upgrade the coffees.

(leaves)

(TREVOR is still momentarily but then starts fidgeting with his collar. He starts straightening out the tablecloth. The WAITER reenters carrying a bottle of champagne and glasses.)

WAITER. Here we go. The house champagne.

(relights candle and fills the champagne glasses)

Much better! Have I forgotten anything?

TREVOR. No, fine, thanks.

WAITER. Excellent!

(As he leaves, he casts a furtive glance at PAULA who enters.)

PAULA. Trevor? What is this?

> (**TREVOR** *shrugs.* **PAULA** *hesitates, then grabs the box.*
> *She tries opening it, but fumbles.*)

TREVOR. Try it with the chair?

> (**PAULA** *sits. Finally opens it. Squeals.*)

PAULA. Oh my god! Trevor!

TREVOR. Paula, will you marry me?

> (**PAULA***'s eyes alight, then … *)

PAULA. *(slowly)* Trevor you know that I would love to marry
you …
> (**TREVOR** *leans across table*)
some day.
> (*She slides the box back to him.*)

TREVOR. Oh.
> (*pause*)
And what day would that be?

PAULA. I was trying to tell you. The Blackberry? I was receiving contract terms.

TREVOR. You're negotiating a contract while I'm proposing to you?

PAULA. It's my dream job Trevor. A promotion.

TREVOR. A promotion … That's good. That's great, you've worked so hard.

PAULA. Thank you Trevor.

> (*beat*)

I was approached.

TREVOR. Approached?

PAULA. By another company.

TREVOR. You were approached by another company. Are you moving out of town?

PAULA. No, I'm going to be your boss.

TREVOR. *(pause)* My boss?!

> (**PAULA** *nods.*)

OK, I think you're a bit confused. I already have a boss. McReynolds –

PAULA. McReynolds has decided to seek outside interests.

TREVOR. Oh.

(*pause*)

So you're my new boss!

PAULA. Yes, and I want you to know how much I am looking forward to working with you.

TREVOR. You just happen to pick this one to be your dream job? My boss?!

PAULA. Trevor, this is the chance of a lifetime for me.

TREVOR. I thought they were going to promote you at LPC.

PAULA. I've been hearing that for two years. They'd never promote me. You know what they told me on my last review?

TREVOR. That you need to work on your people skills.

PAULA. That I need to work on my people skills. Imagine!

TREVOR. Look, Paula, I'm delighted. No one deserves it more than you.

(*pause*)

Couldn't you have waited – My boss! There would have been other jobs. Something just as good –

PAULA. That's so *easy* for you to say!

TREVOR. Now, wait –

PAULA. You know at first I felt bad. I told them they should promote *you* – that I heard they had this really *smart* guy Trevor Palumbo or something and that they should promote him for the job and do you know what they told me?

TREVOR. They, who's they?

PAULA. They, *senior management.* They said, sure he's smart, but he has no focus, no ambition. And he's not a team player. Cutting out of the Christmas party after 25 minutes!

TREVOR. I don't like this.

PAULA. Trevor, try to understand how this would look. What it would do to my career – to both of our careers. You know my strict policy about dating co-workers.

TREVOR. You wouldn't be dating me, we'd be engaged! Engagement is OK ... You're dumping me.

PAULA. Trevor, I'm not dumping you! I love you! ... Look, the dumping is for a good reason. And everything will be fine again once we're no longer working together.

TREVOR. And now I have to find a new job?!

PAULA. No, Trevor!

TREVOR. No?!

PAULA. Look, it's very *easy* for you. Mr. Never had to work a day in your life. Always sent to the finest schools, everything chosen for you by your parents. You've never even had a summer job have you? I don't know why you even have this job. Your family with all their money – the grape juice kings –

TREVOR. Drink. My family produces grape drink.

PAULA. You never had to struggle. My father left us when I was eight. I was the first one in my family to graduate from high school. Not college – high school. You didn't know that. Then four years at Yale on scholarship. Two more years grinding it out at Bain and Company, then business school. Then two years at LPC. That's ten years of my life – and I'm not even counting the spelling bees before that. Ten years vs. the two years we've had! Add it up –

TREVOR. I don't need a calculator.

(**WAITER** *enters humming "Here Comes The Bride".*)

PAULA. I'm sorry.

(leaves)

(Curtain.)

Scene 2

(A very nice corner office. Nice big desk with a flatscreen computer, speakerphone, nice plants, nice artwork and decorations, a large free-standing easel or blackboard filled with obscure business diagramming, an oversized couch for guests. It's a nice day outside – the sun is shining onto the desk and flatscreen.)

*(**PAULA** enters, dressed in business attire and sneakers. She removes her jacket, slowly removes her sneakers and replaces them with business shoes, gets her cup of coffee which is already percolating. She seems tired. She sits, glances through a few papers in her inbox, closes her eyes, reads a bit more. She looks at her computer screen, squints, types in some stuff, squints, types some more, squints. She fiddles with the screen. She gets up and pulls the shade down. However, the shade is semitranslucent and the sun continues to shine brightly onto the computer screen. She squints and types, squints and types, fiddles some more with the screen. Flipping through her Rolodex, she dials. It rings a lot.)*

MAN'S VOICE. Maintenance.

PAULA. Hi, this is Paula LaBrek on 4N. I was in morning meetings my whole first week, so I hadn't noticed this before, but I'm having a little problem with my shade. It doesn't seem to block light very well, which makes seeing my computer screen completely impossible. Could you send someone over to install a new one, a thicker one?

MAN'S VOICE. No ma'am.

PAULA. This is Paula LaBrek … New *Managing Director of Operations* Paula LaBrek. I'm a Level 8.

MAN'S VOICE. Impossible. Company policy. Everyone gets the same shade.

PAULA. Fine, I'll replace it myself then.

MAN'S VOICE. No ma'am. You can't go changing that shade on your own. That's a union job.

PAULA. With whom am I speaking?

MAN'S VOICE. Spencer, Mack Spencer ma'am. 1683V.

PAULA. *(scribbling)* OK Mr. Mack Spencer 1683V. I think I'll just have to go a little over your head here.

MAN'S VOICE. Good luck, ma'am. You're not the first to try. Company policy. They're not going to change them all just for you, Singapore, Tijuana, Bangkok, New York, Tokyo, every shade would have to be changed. Everyone gets the same shade.

PAULA. Oh yeah? We'll see about that.

(other line rings / calm and professional)

Paula LaBrek.

MEXICAN VOICE. This is Tijuana. The shipment, they no here.

PAULA. The heads? The doll heads – we needed those to be there today. Did you contact Singapore? We're going to miss the Christmas season!

MEXICAN VOICE. Sorry, they no heads here.

PAULA. Damn. OK.

(speed-dials)

Answer! Answer!

ASIAN VOICE. Good day, this is Ling in the Singapore shipping office...

PAULA. Hi Ling –

ASIAN VOICE. ...I cannot get to the phone right now, but if –

PAULA. Something's wrong...

*(**PAULA** speed-dials.)*

MELODIOUS FEMALE RECORDING. Hello, this is the technical support hot desk. Please speak your work order number now.

PAULA. I don't have a number!

MELODIOUS FEMALE RECORDING. I'm sorry, I did not get that. Please speak your work order number now.

PAULA. Operator.

MELODIOUS FEMALE RECORDING. I'm sorry, but we cannot find that number.

PAULA. Operator!

MELODIOUS FEMALE RECORDING. I'm sorry, but we cannot find that number

PAULA. Representative?

MELODIOUS FEMALE RECORDING. Please hold while I connect you to a customer service representative.

(Catchy theme song for The Sopranos comes on speakerphone. It plays for a while.)

INDIAN VOICE. This is Patchia. How can I help you?

PAULA. Patchia, this is Paula LaBrek in headquarters.

INDIAN VOICE. Yes, Ms. LaBrek!

PAULA. Listen, is automation screwed up, 'cause we're missing a shipment?

INDIAN VOICE. Yes, Ms. LaBrek! It's the Linux migration – all systems are down. But we're working on it.

PAULA. Again? When will it be back up?

INDIAN VOICE. Soon, very soon, we hope.

PAULA. Soon. Soon we're going to start outsourcing you guys in New Delhi to – to Equatorial Guinea! Now get cracking!

(Another line rings.)

PAULA. *(calm again)* Paula LaBrek.

GAY MAN'S VOICE. Paula, listen, it's Larry. I wanted to let you know this; we're having a little problem with the presentation.

PAULA. A little problem? With the Board Presentation?!

(The other line rings. She glances at the caller ID.)

Holy shit! I'll call you back.

PAULA. *(short staccato breaths, then calm)* Bernard, good morning.

BERNARD. *(calm)* Paula, where are my heads? I have 30,000 Becky Wecky dolls that need their heads.

PAULA. Yes, well, the shipment is delayed.

BERNARD. That's not good Paula. We can't miss the Christmas season.

PAULA. Yes, of course. I just got through to tech. Everything is frozen – it's the Linux migration.

BERNARD. Ah, the Linux migration.

(explodes)

The only thing I see migrating are our customers! Now get me those god damn heads!

(The other line rings.)

PAULA. There are those extras – extra heads – in Singapore warehousing – the Pistol Petes –

BERNARD. Pistol Pete is a commando! And he wears an eyepatch. You can't put a Pistol Pete head on a Becky Wecky. Little girls won't stand for it!

PAULA. No, of course not.

BERNARD. *(sadistically calm again)* Goodbye Paula.

*(**PAULA** picks up the other line which is still ringing.)*

PAULA. *(calm or trying)* Paula LaBrek.

FEMALE VOICE. Paula, where have you been?! Times Roman 12 Paula! You're using Times Roman 12 on the Board Presentation?

PAULA. Oh no.

FEMALE VOICE. Helvetica 10 Paula – you know that. The Board likes Helvetica 10.

PAULA. But I had Helvetica –

FEMALE VOICE. This is $50 million factory Paula! The Board's not going to risk $50 million on Times Roman 12!

PAULA. The print shop – I should have had confirmation –

FEMALE VOICE. Did you check your e-mails?

PAULA. I can't read my e-mails! I need to get a new shade –

FEMALE VOICE. You can't do that.

*(**PAULA** crosses the office, lifts the cumbersome easel and carries it towards the window to block the light.)*

FEMALE VOICE. Did you try calling the print shop?

PAULA. It's Columbus Day. It's closed.

(*Tripping,* **PAULA** *and easel fall to the ground.*)

FEMALE VOICE. Get back to me! I'll be updating my resume.

(**PAULA** *claws back to her feet and resets the easel to block the window.*)

PAULA. (*calmly into speakerphone*) Trevor? Could you come in here please?

(**PAULA** *sits very still at her spacious desk. It would appear his office is quite a distance.*)

(**TREVOR** *enters carrying some papers; he looks anxious. He waits by the door and they look at each other for a moment.*)

PAULA. Would you like to come in?

(**TREVOR** *sits on the oversized couch making him look somewhat small and alone.*)

TREVOR. (*anxious*) I really like, like what you've done with the office.

(*points to easel*)

That's festive!

PAULA. Don't get me started. I once used to dream of having a corner office.

TREVOR. Corners are good! Very safe.

PAULA. Trevor, we have a few issues to discuss. Becky Wecky never made it to Mexico.

TREVOR. (*pause*) That's bad ...

PAULA. Yes it is –

TREVOR. Wait, there are those extra Pistol Petes in Singapore!

PAULA. He's a pirate Trevor with an eyepatch. I need Becky Wecky heads.

TREVOR. Pirate? I thought Pete was a commando?

PAULA. Trevor –

TREVOR. We can still use them. The eyepatch comes

off – and they've both got long hair. Shouldn't be a problem.

PAULA. The eyepatch comes off? Why doesn't anybody tell me these things?

*(***TREVOR*** *shrugs.)*

He has two eyes?

TREVOR. *(Trying to make a joke.)* Yeah, but he can only see out of one. *(Back to work.)* It's really the same doll. But they need to go out today right? Today's a holiday …

PAULA. No … No it isn't! It's not Columbus Day in Singapore. Singapore was discovered by Sherpas. They can pack in the heads *today* along with the plastic dinosaurs.

TREVOR. Right! I'll call Singapore –

PAULA. Don't hurry. I forgot, Linux is down. Everything's frozen.

TREVOR. Not again.

PAULA. It's worse. The board presentation went out in Times Roman.

TREVOR. Oh, man.

PAULA. Nothing we can do. Just wait for Linux. Which is the main reason I've called you in … Trevor, I have a project for you. I think you're going to like it.

TREVOR. A – project?

PAULA. Yes, I need someone to spearhead this Linux migration. Someone to ride herd on tech.

TREVOR. Well, Paula, I'm not sure – how about Fredo? He was an engineer –

PAULA. No, I don't think you understand. This project's *high exposure.*

TREVOR. Oh, right. Then Priscilla, she'd be –

PAULA. No, Trevor, I'm putting *you* on this project.

TREVOR. Oh, I see, I'm certainly flattered –

PAULA. This will be good for you – good for your career. If you solve this Linux issue, senior management is going to notice. I'll make sure of it.

TREVOR. Well, um, you see that's the problem. I sort of prefer low, or maybe medium's OK. Medium exposure is fine with me.

PAULA. Trevor! What is *wrong* with you? Everyone else would jump at this project.

TREVOR. Well maybe I'm not like everyone else. There's something I have to tell you –

PAULA. You know what your problem is? You're afraid of success.

TREVOR. I most certainly am not!

PAULA. Yes you are.

TREVOR. No, I'm *not.*

PAULA. You are afraid. It's just like your agoraphobia.

TREVOR. I do not have agoraphobia. I don't like being *alone* in public places. That's not an accredited phobia.

PAULA. Trevor, what are you doing here? Do you want to stay in your cube for the rest of your life? Where's it going to end?

TREVOR. Where's it going to end? Yeah, where? So you give me this great big project. And so I ace it, then what happens? I get noticed by the higher ups? By *senior management*? Then they put me on some even higher exposure projects. And then what – a promotion? More hours? Higher and higher exposure projects. Until something screws up and I eventually come crashing down!

PAULA. *(pause)* So what's the alternative Trevor? Leaving the corporate world? Going home to work for your parents' company?

TREVOR. They don't want that. That's got its own stresses.

PAULA. Everything's stressful Trevor! That's life. You can't keep escaping life.

TREVOR. So what – so I succeed at this project. *Then* I'm living life?

PAULA. You're living life so long as you're doing something, struggling. It's never a given that you're going to succeed in anything.

TREVOR. Oh, so I'm going to fail? You're setting me up to fail? So you can get me out of your group?

PAULA. Trevor! Have you just decided to go insane? Don't you see why I'm doing this? You've got all the abilities to succeed. I believe in you Trevor!

TREVOR. *(hands over paper)* I just finished this.

PAULA. *(reading)* ... While our days together may have been brief in number, I will always cherish – What? – Therefore, with a heart heavy with regret, it behooves me to inform you – Trevor, is this a resignation letter? You're quitting? ... You're going to LPC? What?

TREVOR. That's right.

PAULA. My old job? This sounds like my old job. Trevor, why?

TREVOR. I was *approached*. The position was vacant.

PAULA. But that's a lateral, a lateral – that's the easy way out. Nobody leaves for a lateral.

TREVOR. Well I do. I already signed the contract.

PAULA. Well unsign it. Trevor think of what you're doing, think of your career.

TREVOR. It could lead to a promotion.

PAULA. Yeah, that's what they told me too when I took that job. It's still a lateral – that's not going to look good.

TREVOR. I thought you'd be happy.

PAULA. Trevor, I really cannot have you – not for me – I can't have you harming your career for me.

TREVOR. My career is my business. I'm not a child. Maybe it's not my career that you're so concerned about. Maybe it's your career! That's all you've ever cared about. Now who's going to do your little Linux project?

PAULA. That's a low blow Trevor! What's gotten into you? Am I really that horrible? You just can't wait – can't wait to get away from me. Is that it Trevor?

TREVOR. Yes! – No! You see what these jobs are doing to

us!

(exits)

PAULA. *(longish pause)* Yes. Yes, I do.

(Curtain.)

(During the transition between Scenes 2 and 3, we hear the following recorded messages on Paula's voicemail)

INDIAN VOICE. Miss LaBrek! Mis LaBrek!! I know it's been a while, but we are now extremely close, very close indeed on the Linux migration. It may be the wireless interface. Not to worry, we are on it!

FEMALE VOICE. Paula! Where are you? The plastic dinosaurs. Did Triceratops wear an eye patch?

GAY MAN'S VOICE. Paula, it's Larry. We have this problem, it's with the XV-18 reports. They seem to have arrived this month in landscape formatting. The XV-18s need to be in portrait. Bernard is very concerned.

CALM MAN'S VOICE. Paula. It's Bernard. I noticed some strange thing on my desk today. It looked a bit like the XV-18 report, except for some reason it was in landscape. I'm confused Paula. Oh, and by the way, when you get a moment, why don't you get on my calendar? I believe your 6-month review is coming up.

Scene 3

(Six months later, early evening. **PAULA** *is sitting alone in same corner table as Scene 1. She looks somewhat different from the earlier scenes, somewhat sexier in both her hairstyle and clothing. The table is set for two with champagne glasses. She fidgets a bit.)*

*(***TREVOR*** *enters, dressed a bit more formally than prior scenes, in a conservative business suit. He looks nervous and a bit disheveled.)*

TREVOR. Paula?

PAULA. Trevor. Trevor.

TREVOR. You look great.

PAULA. You don't look too awful yourself.

(They look at each other for a long awkward moment. **TREVOR** *remains standing.)*

PAULA. *(rising)* Here let me fix this.

(She straightens out his tie, fixes his hair.)

TREVOR. Oh, no, thanks ...

(notices champagne)

Hey, what's this for?

PAULA. I thought we should celebrate. I heard about your promotion.

TREVOR. *(shrugs)* Oh ... well, thanks.

*(***PAULA*** *reseats herself.* **TREVOR** *follows and moves his setting so that it's next to hers catty-corner in the corner and sits. A shorter awkward moment and he abruptly kisses her on the cheek. She was expecting a bit more. This too is awkward.)*

PAULA. *(lifting her glass)* To Trevor Palumbo. To your new promotion. To your success.

TREVOR. *(lifting glass)* To *our* success. *(he feels uncomfortable and starts to go)* This is a bad idea.

PAULA. I would also like to apologize. I was wrong about you.

TREVOR. Wrong?

PAULA. Those things I said before you left. I'm so sorry.

TREVOR. No Paula. You were right! I *was* afraid of success. And I was taking the easy way out.

PAULA. Well, you sure showed me. You showed everyone. Two years I was at LPC and nothing. And you promoted in six months. On the fast track.

TREVOR. Nah, they just realized they blew it with you. I lucked out ... So, how's it going with you?

PAULA. Oh, fine, fine.

TREVOR. That's good ... Linux, did they get that fixed?

PAULA. Oh, yes. Linux is fine. But now we've gone wireless. Now the system crashes whenever anyone turns on a cellphone or a toaster oven. Oh, and another presentation got out with Times Roman.

TREVOR. Well, you know what they say, Rome wasn't made in a day.

PAULA. Trevor, I'm not building Rome. All I'm trying to do is protect 15 measly share points ... What else is going on? Outside of work.

TREVOR. I don't know. Not much. My dad finally retired.

PAULA. He did? So now your mom's got him hanging around the house?

TREVOR. Yeah, she's trying to get him to take up some hobbies. Golf, gardening, skydiving, whatever.

PAULA. And how about you Trevor? Are you up to anything, yourself, outside of work?

TREVOR. Me, no. Just work, work, work! ... And you?

PAULA. Work, work, work!

(*They share a nervous laugh.*)

So ... I suppose we can be friends again. Right?

TREVOR. Sure, friends or close acquaintances, that would be OK.

PAULA. (*pause*) Oh.

(*The Blackberry goes off.* **PAULA** *removes it from her*

purse, hesitates, then violently throws it at the wall. She then opens her menu)

TREVOR. Hey!

(He rises to retrieve the Blackberry and moves to hand it to her.)

PAULA. These specials look very appealing.

TREVOR. *(studying Blackberry)* You might want to read this.

(he puts it in front of her, she pushes it away)

PAULA. Not interested.

(Trevor again puts it back in front of her, she pushes it away)

PAULA. Maybe we should get an appetizer –

*(**TREVOR** places the Blackberry in her face – she glances at it.)*

A merger?

(scrolling down message)

You guys are buying us out?!

TREVOR. I guess so.

PAULA. Trevor, a merger! Do you realize what this means? We're going to be working at the same company again!

(inspecting him)

You knew about this didn't you.

TREVOR. I heard rumors.

PAULA. Rumors … Oh … Oh!

TREVOR. What?

PAULA. What's your title at LPC?

TREVOR. Titles don't really matter.

PAULA. Yes, they *do* matter. You're the Managing Director of Operations and I'm the Managing Director of Operations. Two Managing Directors of Operations. Two. They don't need two.

TREVOR. You don't know that.

PAULA. I'm through. Fired.

TREVOR. Paula, you're not going to be fired.

PAULA. Yeah? How do *you* know?

TREVOR. I just do.

PAULA. Oh. Oh, of course, why shouldn't you know? LPC is the buyer. You're the predator, I'm the prey ... Oh ...

TREVOR. Paula...

PAULA *(cont.)* *(realizing)* You're going to be my boss. Of course, you've just been promoted and if I'm not going to be fired, then obviously I'm going to report to you. Well, I don't mind. It's a shock, but I'll adjust.

TREVOR. Paula –

PAULA. No, you deserve this Trevor. You really do. After all those things I said to you. How ironic!

TREVOR. Paula, all those things you said were true. You were right. You helped me! I was completely sheltered. I had no direction. No ambition.

PAULA. I was horrible to you. Putting my career before us. My career!

TREVOR. No, you were right all along. Everything you've accomplished you did on your own. But I've always done things the easy way, doing whatever my parents want. Well no longer!

PAULA. I always knew you could do it once you set your mind to it.

TREVOR. I was the one who was wrong Paula. Not you. Personal relationships are important, yes, but not everything. Sometimes, unfortunately, business must come first.

PAULA. I understand.

TREVOR. No you don't. But no matter what, I want you to know how I feel about you Paula. I'm still in love with you. I always have loved you. And I always will. No matter what.

PAULA. And I love you. Always.

(She reaches for him and they share a real kiss. As they part, **TREVOR** *is crying.)*

PAULA. Trevor, it's OK.

TREVOR. Damned allergies.

(inspects menu)

PAULA. You know what, I'll look for another job just like you did.

TREVOR. What!?

PAULA. Yes, I think this is a good thing Trevor. For me too. I've been thinking about quitting this corporate rat race ever since you left. Maybe I can do something with my accounting background in a smaller company. Someplace where I can actually *do* something. Build something. Make a difference. *(New idea.)* You know how I love cooking. Maybe I can go culinary school. Open my own pastry shop or a restaurant. Who knows?

TREVOR. No, Paula, you can't throw away all you've accomplished.

PAULA. Who says I can't? I can do whatever I want! I'm an adult.

TREVOR. Paula, you have to be rational. And realistic.

PAULA. I *choose* to be irrational. I choose to be unrealistic! You may be my boss, but you don't run my life.

TREVOR. I'm not going to be your boss. I've quit.

PAULA. Quit?

TREVOR. Yes quit. Thanks to you. Thanks to your advice. You know I was never cut out for the corporate life-style.

PAULA. What are you talking about? You're a big success.

TREVOR. Paula, you've got the job. You're the last Managing Director of Operations standing.

PAULA. Well I don't want that shitty job! … Don't tell me you quit for me? … Trevor?!

TREVOR. No Paula, I didn't just quit for you! It's not always about you.

PAULA. Fine.

TREVOR. Fine.

PAULA. No, not fine! You can't just quit Trevor. Nobody just quits!

TREVOR. I've decided to work for my family's business. OK? I told you my father finally retired. …That's all I have to say.

PAULA. Oh … Well, that's great.

TREVOR. Thanks! *(avoiding her)* I'm hungry. Where the hell's our waiter. Where is everyone? *(He avoids her and looks at the menu intently.)*

PAULA. *(muttering)* Agoraphobia.

TREVOR. What?

PAULA. Let's order.

TREVOR. Yes let's.

(short awkward pause – she knows he hasn't told her something, and he knows she knows)

PAULA. What's wrong? … Why won't you look at me?

TREVOR. I'm going to get the chicken pot pie.

PAULA. Trevor…

TREVOR. Nothing's wrong. It's just that I'll be busy. Very busy. Things are very demanding. Some folks are keyed up. I've got to prove myself.

PAULA. Oh. I see.

TREVOR. I thought you, that you wouldn't approve.

PAULA. Trevor, you have nothing to be ashamed of. Children all around the country rely on your family's product as an important part of their daily nutritional value … *(pause.)*

TREVOR. Paula, my family's business may be a bit more complicated than you think.

PAULA. I thought they made grape drink.

TREVOR. They *do* make grape drink. But there's other things too. Bottling, distilleries, some other things. Things not so nice. Racketeering, extortion, heroin, gun-running, organ-harvesting … Things like that …

(pause)

You see? I shouldn't have done that. Bad business practice.

(long pause)

Say something!

PAULA. I'm supposed to say something. So, you're telling me you're what … involved with the mob?

TREVOR. *(winces)* No, not the mob, Paula. I'm with the Mafia.

*(**PAULA** bolts for the door, chair flying, drinks spilling. **TREVOR** tries to stop her, with both falling to the floor.)*

PAULA. Get off me! Maniac!

TREVOR. Only if you promise to listen. To hear me out … Paula please! …

PAULA. OK, OK, I'll listen.

(He releases her and she immediately bolts for the door again. He tackles her again.)

TREVOR. Paula, I can't let you go. Not like this.

PAULA. OK, OK, you win.

TREVOR. Now promise me you'll come back to the table and have a civilized conversation.

PAULA. OK, I promise.

*(He hesitantly releases her. This time she slowly returns back to the table with **TREVOR** positioning himself between her and the exit. He recovers the chair for her and she sits.)*

TREVOR. *(calmly seating himself)* You see Paula all my life I've been living a lie. My parents didn't want their lifestyle for me. They wanted something "better" something "legitimate." They sheltered me. But inside, I always wanted to be like my father. I wanted the excitement, the *real* life drama, *real* challenges, not this mind-numbing corporate cube existence.

PAULA. Ah, I see.

TREVOR. But each time I tried to get in, they kept pushing me out! …

PAULA. Ah ha.

TREVOR. You were totally right what you told me. I *was* afraid. Afraid to accept what I really am. Afraid to stand up to my parents. Even afraid to tell you all about this. Afraid you wouldn't want to go out with – with someone like me. But you opened my eyes. You gave me courage.

PAULA. *(pause)* You know, it's funny, but you don't look like the Mafia type.

TREVOR. I know. I know that. Eight years at the Happy Friends Day School, that takes a toll on your reputation. But it's what's inside that counts.

PAULA. So my boyfriend – ex-boyfriend. Who I've known for what – two and a half years – is really a Mafioso inside?

TREVOR. I know and I'm sorry. Maybe two and a half years isn't enough to really know someone after all. But I think I know you Paula. Paula, I know you. That counts for something.

PAULA. But I don't know you. Not at all. Who exactly are you Trevor Palum – Palumbo. Palumbo.
Palumbo as in the Palumbo Crime Family. *That* Palumbo?!

TREVOR. *(winces)* Yes, that Palumbo.

PAULA. Mug Chop! Mug Chop Palumbo!?

TREVOR. No, no, that's my dad. I'm still just Trevor. And Mug Chop's just what the tabloids call him. Sells more papers. His real name is Maxwell.

PAULA. You're the son of Mug Chop Palumbo!

TREVOR. Yes, but it's probably not best to call him that – not to his face. He's sensitive about that.

PAULA. Trevor, this is for real. This is legit!

TREVOR. Legit? Well, some of it. The grape drink.

PAULA. No, I mean you're really – why haven't you ever told me?

TREVOR. I don't know. I'm not supposed to talk about it … You never asked.

(The Blackberry goes off again. It keeps buzzing. **PAULA** *is very intense.* **TREVOR** *looks worried.*

After a while the Blackberry turns off. Long pause.)

PAULA. Let's do it!

TREVOR. Do what?

PAULA. The Mafia thing. I'd like to join.

TREVOR. What?! No, I don't think so.

PAULA. Why not?

TREVOR. No, no, trust me. It's not for you.

PAULA. What is it too *dangerous?*

TREVOR. No, not dangerous. But stressful. Yes, it can be very stressful.

PAULA. But Trevor I'm great at handling stress. That and spreadsheets. I'm the master of stress.

TREVOR. Paula, you're being ridiculous.

PAULA. I'm serious! I want in! I'm fed up with all of it. All the endless meetings, all the stupid computer upgrades. I'd be great at it, no bureaucracy, no red tape –

TREVOR. Oh, don't be so sure about that. There's plenty of bureaucracy in the Mafia. Lots of red tape. Ever since RICO –

PAULA. Look, I can start with regular stuff. Maybe you need a good accountant.

TREVOR. Well, that's actually kind of funny. We do need –

PAULA. Trevor, you know I'm a whiz at accounting – And I like cooking. I'll cook the books for you! You need that right?

TREVOR. No, no, impossible. You're not suitable.

PAULA. Come on Trevor. It'll be sexy.

TREVOR. Sexy?

PAULA. Us getting out of the corporate rat race, that's sexy!

TREVOR. Paula, please –

PAULA. My mobster!

(She kisses him fiercely. He at first resists. Then can't. The kiss lasts a while.)

WAITER. *(entering, nervous, clears throat)* You're Trevor Palumbo right?

TREVOR. Yes –

WAITER. Excellent.

*(**TREVOR** and the **WAITER** both pull out guns. **TREVOR** is shot. They grapple, the table collapses, with the **WAITER** on top. **PAULA** is watching. She reaches for the steak knife. She plunges it into the **WAITER**. And again. And again. And AGAIN! There's lots of blood.*

She stops and looks at the two corpses.)

PAULA. Trevor!

*(She lifts **TREVOR** and shakes him.)*

Trevor!

TREVOR. *(opening his eyes)* Shit …

(smiles)

That was *excellent*! … Thank you. Thank you for doing that.

PAULA. Trevor!

(kisses him a lot)

Oh, my god. Trevor, don't move.

TREVOR. *(lifting himself up)* No, no just a flesh wound.

(grimaces)

Maybe a little more, but I'll be OK… . That was really clever going with the waiter.

PAULA. *(breathing hard)* Trevor, you need a, a … he's dead right?

TREVOR. Oh, yes. Quite dead.

PAULA. Trevor, you need …

(catching her breath)

ambulance. You need …

(trying to catch her breath)

TREVOR. Nah, don't worry. I really didn't want to get you involved. Thank you Paula, I will never forget this. This gives me a warm feeling. Now they're going to think twice. Yes, sir! After his little problem they're going to think twice about disrespecting me. Now who says I haven't earned my position? Huh? Anybody? See, I told you it's not good to be alone in public places.

(PAULA *meanwhile has been wheezing, gasping for air. She faces the audience, arms outstretched at her sides, covered in blood. Her eyes appear glazed. She's coughing, almost retching.*)

Paula?

PAULA. *(in between gasps)* … in shock …

TREVOR. *(holding her)* In shock? No, I don't think you're really in shock. Let me see your hands.

(grabs her hands)

See this – your killing hand? Steady as a rock. And this is only your first time, right?

PAULA. I'm in shock!

TREVOR. And you see that's a full sentence. People in shock don't talk like that. I think you might have a knack for this.

PAULA. *(wide-eyed)* A knack … for killing?!

TREVOR. No Paula! Not just killing … there's spreadsheets – and other things. Lots of other things! I think we could make a great team. Paula, will you marry me? …

(PAULA*'s eyes remain open wide.*)

And the job! The job too. We need talent like you …

(PAULA*'s eyes remain wide.*)

Consiglieri? How's that sound? … And 50% of the grape drink factory? … the whole grape drink factory … Please Paula! Please!

(PAULA *fiercely embraces* TREVOR, *causing him to wince. The theme song for The Sopranos comes on again.*)

(Curtain.)

THE GERBIL

CHARACTERS

JAMES	40's
DOG	20's-30's, a black man
MARGARET	40's, James' wife

SETTING

A nice dining-room.

TIME

The present.

*(Curtain opens on an upscale dining room. It's night and, if visible, a wall clock reads 2:50 a.m. The room is furnished nicely, if a bit eclectically, with a cabinet containing drawers and fine china and silver along with some decorations, family photos, some African masks and carved animals near the door, etc. There is one door to the room, currently open, through which some light seeps into the dining room. Seated at the table is **JAMES**, a man of indeterminate middle-age. He is wearing silk pajamas and eating ice cream out of a container. In between bites, he hums a bit, the "birthday song.")*

*(A muffled crash is heard. A black man **DOG**, 20s or 30s, dressed ninja-like in black ski mask, drops from the ceiling among broken glass. **JAMES** falls out of his chair and retreats to the dining room door.)*

*(**DOG** takes a step forward. **JAMES** retreats further, thrashing about and yanking open drawers from the dining room cabinet, removing a large carving knife. Standing between **DOG** and the door, he brandishes the knife. **DOG** is careful to keep the table between himself and **JAMES**.)*

*(Brandishing the knife with more confidence, **JAMES** moves along the table with **DOG** mirroring his moves on the other side. There is a cordless phone on the table. **JAMES** moves for the phone, but **DOG** is quicker.)*

*(**DOG** pushes the table towards **JAMES**, nearly knocking him over. **JAMES** pushes back but with one hand holding the knife finds himself pushed nearly out of the dining room, with the table now wedged near the door. **JAMES** can't get at **DOG** with the knife, while **DOG** remains trapped in the room. **DOG** rummages through the drawers and removes another knife, one noticeably larger than **JAMES'**. **JAMES** rushes out of the room. **DOG** hesitates momentarily, then pushes the table aside and chases after him.)*

(We hear some noises off-stage. Moments later **DOG** *returns to the kitchen followed by* **JAMES**, *now carrying a gun.)*

JAMES. *(turning on light)* So, you've lost the arms race. Now give me that phone.

DOG. I can't do that.

JAMES. I said to give me the phone.

DOG. I don't mean no disrespect. It was just the silver. That's all I wanted. Just silver man.

JAMES. I'll shoot you.

(He readies his aim.)

DOG. I can't go back to no prison. Please.

JAMES. Prison is where you belong. I'm going to count to three. One …

DOG. No please.

JAMES. Two …

DOG. *(starting to cry)* Please …

JAMES. Thr –

DOG. No wait! Think! Maybe we can make a deal. A win-win.

JAMES. *(beat)* What can I win?

DOG. I don't know. Anything you like! I got a lot of skills. I'm an excellent burglar. Real excellent.

JAMES. It doesn't look that way to me.

DOG. This don't count man. No offense, but you don't got no business being up this late. And the piece? This is a fluke. A real fluke.

JAMES. Oh, so you think it's a fluke huh? A fluke! You don't even know who you're dealing with do you?

DOG. No, no man. I didn't mean it like that.

JAMES. Do you know who I am?

DOG. I don't know man. You somebody famous? I think maybe I seen you.

JAMES. Oh?

DOG. I don't know. You that guy? Hollywood Squares! You that dude in bottom corner.

JAMES. Hollywood Squares?

DOG. No, man, wait. That guy in the movie theaters ... The Cellphone Man! Is that you?

JAMES. I'm Senator Billings.

DOG. You a *Senator*? Shit!

JAMES. You know you really should do a bit of research. Don't you do any, what do you call it, casing of your jobs?

DOG. Sure man, I do that. I'm a professional. You don't see me setting off no alarms do you? It don't matter who the house belongs, you was supposed to be asleep.

JAMES. Well it appears that I'm awake.

(readies gun)

DOG. No wait! I'll do anything. Anything you like! I can't do prison again.

JAMES. *(pause)* Anything?

DOG. Yes, absolutely!

JAMES. OK, then. I'd like you to kill my wife.

DOG. *(pause)* No, come on ...

*(**JAMES** readies gun)*

Are you serious? Are you serious about this?

JAMES. I'm serious. She's sleeping upstairs. Shouldn't be difficult.

DOG. I don't think you understand. I'm a burglar, not a murderer. That's a whole separate category. I don't know first thing how to kill nobody.

JAMES. Just an idea.

(readies gun)

DOG. Why me?

JAMES. You've already broken into the house. It's a neat arrangement.

DOG. But that's serious shit man. Killing your wife? She really that bad?

JAMES. None of your business.

DOG. You right, you right … It's just that you know, seeing that I'm not an assassin, that ain't my trade. You know, it might help me if you give me a reason, something not to like her.

JAMES. I found a pair of men's socks in the bedroom last week. Athletic socks, white ones with a red stripe, a red stripe, like the kind I wore in third grade. But definitely a man's size. She says it was a mistake with the laundry service, but I don't believe her.

DOG. Socks? You gonna to kill her over a pair of socks?

JAMES. She's also trying to blackmail me.

DOG. Shit! What she doing that for?

JAMES. A variety of things. I've had a few indiscretions of my own. About 13 if I count correctly. That's only one for every two years of marriage. A few were men, or maybe boys, I have a don't ask don't tell policy when it comes to that. Regardless, the constituents won't like it. And there were a few … clubs, a few clubs I forced her to go to with me – I figured it would help me cut down on the indiscretions. She kept the receipts. Satisfied?

DOG. Sorry.

JAMES. Actually, I think *you* look a little familiar. You go to clubs?

DOG. No man. I work at night. I don't go to no clubs.

JAMES. Take off that mask.

DOG. No, no, I can't do that. I ain't never take off the mask. I can't do that.

JAMES. *(pointing gun)* Prepare to die.

(DOG *abruptly tears off the mask, revealing a conservative nicely-trimmed haircut.*)

JAMES. *(inspecting him closely)* Mmm. OK, let's get this over with.

DOG. I don't know man. How you propose we do this?

JAMES. I don't propose *we* do anything. This is *your* job. You've already broken into the house, without tripping any alarms as you point out. Now all you need is to go up the stairs and fulfill your end of the bargain.

DOG. And then you'll let me go?

JAMES. That's right.

DOG. How'm I supposed to kill her?

JAMES. Why not just smother her with a pillow – no, that's not so good. Better to make it look like a struggle, like she caught you trying to steal the silverware.

DOG. Stealing silverware in her bedroom?

JAMES. Jewelry then. She's got a ton of the stuff up there. Come to think about it, you'd better take some of it with you. That way it'll look like a real robbery gone bad. I could use the insurance money.

DOG. Couldn't we stick with the silver? I don't know jewelry. My fence, he won't touch the stuff.

JAMES. Take some of both if that makes you feel better.

DOG. OK then!

(starts inspecting the silver in the cabinet)

JAMES. First kill. Then steal.

DOG. I'll need a weapon. How about your gun?

JAMES. I keep the gun. Besides it doesn't make any sense for you to kill her with my gun. Take the knife.

DOG. I should just stab her in her sleep?

JAMES. She's not a vampire. At least not classically defined. It's best to make it look like a struggle.

DOG. And then I can take the silver and you let me go?

JAMES. That's right.

DOG. Well in that case, would it be OK if I inspect your collection first? I may not be able to evaluate so good after, you know, all the excitement.

JAMES. Three items. Then let's get going.

DOG. Deal.

(starts opening drawers and doors in the cabinet, inspecting pieces)

Family pieces?

JAMES. *(dismissive)* Wife's stuff. No idea.

DOG. Not bad. You know you got some 19th century Flemish? I knew they'd be good shit here.

(picks out a tray and places it on the table)

JAMES. Looks like you really know your stuff. Too bad you don't use those smarts for something productive.

DOG. Well, truth is they always said I test real good in school, but I could never do all that sittin'. Rules out the desk jobs. I once tried the poker, you know professional gambling – but that took more sittin' than the desk job. I think I got the adult A.D.D. Plus I'm an insomniac so I'm up at night anyway. No, I'm gonna stick with the silver.

JAMES. Suit yourself.

DOG. *(picking out another piece)* How about you? You like being a senator?

JAMES. I like the speaking fees. Actually being a senator is easy – the legislative aides do all the work. No the hard part is *running* for senator. This current election in particular. Gallop has me down by eleven points. But it's still early. Back in '98 I was behind by thirteen points at this point, but won by three.

DOG. I would have voted for you, 'cept at the time I was in prison.

JAMES. Thanks. How long were you incarcerated? If you don't mind my asking.

DOG. Six months the first time, three years the second.

JAMES. That's interesting. How did you get caught?

DOG. I ain't *never* been caught. I'm not counting tonight obviously. It's the follow-up where they get you. The first time my fence ratted me out – I'm much more careful nowadays. I do a full screen, including three reference checks. The second time it was my bitch ratted me. Actually we're back together.

JAMES. You got back together with her after she ratted on you? You're a lot more forgiving than I'd be.

DOG. Yes, I can see that … no offense meant Senator.

(inspects a tea set and a goblet)

JAMES. Some taken. Let's hurry this up.

*(**DOG** chooses the goblet.)*

I always found that one too ornate for my tastes.

DOG. It's Rococo you know.

JAMES. *(stopping abruptly)* Wait! … Where's your bag?

DOG. My what?

JAMES. Your bag, satchel, what you use to carry the silver.

DOG. What, no I don't use no satchel.

JAMES. *(slowly leveling the gun)* Oh, so you just walk out, carrying all these items around in in your arms?

DOG. No man, I don't do that. That's too obvious. Satchel, that's too obvious too man. Classy joints like this one, they all got bags I can use. Good plastic bags.

JAMES. Plastic bags? You expect me to believe that?

DOG. What, you don't got no bags?

JAMES. Yes, we have bags. Where else do you think we put the garbage.

DOG. In the kitchen right? Under the sink?

*(**JAMES** continues to look at **DOG**.)*

What you got? You use the Cinch-sack?

JAMES. I don't know. Hefty something –

DOG. Yeah, that's it! That's the one. Hefty Cinch-sack. I knew it. Classy joint like this one. Ain't nothin beat that Cinch-sack! Don't need to double bag, nothin. Could you get me a couple?

JAMES. *(looking carefully at **DOG**)* No, I'm not going to get you any damn Cinch-sack. You can go get your own Cinch-sack once we're done. Knife.

(beat)

Hey. Pull up your pants.

DOG. What? What you talking about? Oh, man, no don't

please. Don't make me do this. I don't do no clubs
man!

(**DOG** *starts to undo his belt.*)

JAMES. Idiot! I said *up*! Pull your pants *up*. I want to see
your socks.

DOG. What you saying man?

JAMES. Your socks. I notice you're wearing white socks.

DOG. So?

JAMES. So why is a burglar dressed all in black wearing
white socks? I bet those socks have a red stripe on the
top. Don't they!

DOG. No man. They just comfortable. Don't got no stripes.

(**JAMES** *motions with the gun and* **DOG** *lifts his pants
leg. The socks have no stripes.* **JAMES** *hesitates, looks
confused.*)

JAMES. All right then. It's cool. That's what you say right.

(*beat*)

Now get the knife.

(*motions with gun*)

DOG. (*picks up the knife*) Don't you got no kids? Won't they
miss their mother?

JAMES. We have a daughter. April. Currently serving in
the Peace Corp. In Gambia, or is it Gabon? I can't
remember.

(*motions dismissively to African masks and carvings*)

Brought us those weird masks up top. Sure she'll miss
her mother. Maybe I'll buy her a new BMW with some
of the insurance money when she gets back. That
should ease her pain.

DOG. (*to picture of blonde girl on wall*) That her?

JAMES. Yeah that's April.

DOG. Man, she's hot!

(*on* **JAMES**)

I mean objectively speaking. *(pause)* Yo, these masks are tight!

JAMES. Enough stalling.

DOG. Wait! Wait a minute! You mentioned you're in an election. Maybe I could break into your opponent's house instead? Bug him, get some dirt on him?

JAMES. My opponent is an out of the closet gay and occasional cross-dresser. Any more dirt I can dredge up on him only solidifies his base. Now move it.

(MARGARET, of indeterminate middle-age, enters, wearing a provocative nightgown. Everyone is startled.)

MARGARET. James?

JAMES. This is a burglar! I just caught him trying to steal our fine silver!

MARGARET. It sounded like you were having some kind of discussion.

DOG. *(slight pause)* Your husband don't like you very much. He wants me to kill you in exchange for my freedom.

(Everyone is silent. Then MARGARET lets out a soft giggle, which slowly grows into a laugh.)

MARGARET. You see? I told you the marriage counseling wasn't working!

MARGARET. You, robber, do you have a name?

DOG. I'd rather not say.

(MARGARET nods, considering, then leaves the room.)

JAMES. Bitch.

(JAMES and DOG retain their positions, unsure. MARGARET returns, armed with her own gun, a duplicate to that of JAMES.)

(Throughout following, MARGARET and JAMES should flaunt and toy with their guns as appropriate. As needed, they could also lip-synch/mouth whatever the other is saying to DOG.)

DOG. Man, this house just-full-a-guns!

MARGARET. Don't you think you should have known that

before you decided to break in? Don't you *case* your jobs?

JAMES. *(nodding)* That's what I told him.

MARGARET. *(carelessly flaunting gun)* I'm sorry, I didn't catch your name.

DOG. Don't got no name. Just dog.

MARGARET. Dog? OK. Now Dog, first I'd like to thank you very much for that handy piece of information. I'm just wondering though, how precisely were you two planning on killing me?

DOG. Don't know. Honest, don't know ma'am. Your husband, the Senator, he had it all planned out. I just wanted the silver. That's it.

MARGARET. Senator?

> *(beat)*

> *This*

> *(pointing at* **JAMES***)*

> is a cutlery salesman!

JAMES. *(softly)* No.

MARGARET. He's hopped up on Viagra and Johnny Walker Red.

> *(to* **JAMES***)*

> You're delusional!

> *(back to* **DOG***)*

> He thinks we're still in role play.

> *(Slowly, she starts a slinky dance, rubbing her gun up and down her thigh, spot on Marilyn Monroe)*

> Happy birthday … Mr. Senator. Happy birthday to you.

> *(vicious)*

> Incompetent! You and this *dog* trying to kill me. What in my sleep, was that it this time? You think I could sleep through all this racket? Coward!

JAMES. *(mostly to* **DOG***)* How much is a man going to take!

MARGARET. The Senator, that's his favorite. Except now,

he can't even get it up with that! What else you need,
Mr. Senator, you want some Levitra too? Maybe some
Ex-Lax to go with?

JAMES. You, frigid bitch –

DOG. I really don't need no silver –

JAMES. *(waiving gun)* How bout you, Mr. Dog? You're a real
robber, right? If you were married to a shrew like this
wouldn't you need a little extra help?

MARGARET. Oh, so now you're bringing him into it? Just
like with April, huh? Can't fight your own battles,
coward?

JAMES. Me? You're the one that told April, about … you
know …

MARGARET. No, I don't. Why don't you tell me you impotent little sociopath. I think Dog here would like to
know too.

DOG. No, no –

JAMES. 21 years ago. 21 years!

MARGARET. I've *always* been faithful to you.

JAMES. Faithful to making my life a living hell.

MARGARET. *(to DOG)* He's right you know. It was only one
indiscretion. All he could muster was one measly indiscretion, but one especially well-suited for him.

(closer to DOG)

What did he tell you?

DOG. Nothin. Didn't tell me nothin. Just that he was a
Senator –

MARGARET. This

(motions wildly around the house)

all this is mine! He's a nobody. Senator!

DOG. I believe you!

(JAMES points the gun.)

Both of you! You're both right … In your own way.

MARGARET. *(to DOG)* I suppose he didn't tell you who I am.

(proud)

I'm Margaret Heyworth.

*(**DOG** is nonplussed.)*

Of Margaret Heyworth Cutlery? … Third largest mall chain in the country?

DOG. Oh, yeah! Yeah, I know that. That's good stuff. I got a Christmas present once, my godmother, got me one of those,

(sizing with hands)

what do you call it the little one with the pointy sides?

JAMES. The medium-serrated. I think that's the medium-serrated.

MARGARET. You think? After 25 years! No wonder you can't meet your sales target.

*(to **DOG**)*

See, he's my husband, but he also works for me. I'm the one who built this brand from the ground up.

(beat)

Do you want to know how we met?

*(**DOG** frozen, then nods)*

In high-school. During the summer. We both started out *the same*, but he's lazy, he has no initiative. And he drinks, well you know that already. And the drugs. And the gambling! His gambling almost did in the entire business. That's when I put in the post-nup.

JAMES. It didn't used to be. It didn't always used to. Remember, at first. We were happy …

MARGARET. Oh, we were happy all right. Until you spoiled it!

JAMES. *(to **DOG**)* 21 years ago. 21 fucking years!

MARGARET. Sweetheart, I don't totally blame you. You were handsome back then, see I can say that. You don't think I married you for your brains do you? And I know, at least back then, before you know, the surgery,

I wasn't the prettiest girl on the block. You had a lot of choices back then. Heck I felt lucky! How does that make you feel?

(**JAMES** *looks touched, starts to say something*)

But all you are now is a delusional impotent loser. But *then, then* you had choices. And what choice did you make?

(*beat*)

I actually wouldn't have minded. You see! I actually *expected* you'd have someone.

(*to* **DOG**)

That's the way with men right?

(*beat*)

But the choice. The choice … that … skank! … That clerk!

JAMES. Assistant manager. She was an assistant manager.

MARGARET. Orange Julius! That's not even retail. That's not even on the fucking directory!

JAMES. (*to* **DOG**) You see? 21 years! Could you take 21 years? Orange Julius this. Orange Julius that! 21 fucking years!

MARGARET. Well, maybe, maybe it wasn't just Orange Julius … Your choice. Of location. The storeroom. *My fucking* storeroom!

JAMES. Where else? Where else do you think we could go? The storeroom was *empty*. It wasn't even knives then. Just spoons. It was *my* idea remember, about the knives. *My* idea about the titanium plating!

MARGARET. (*softly*) I should have left you right then.

JAMES. (*softly*) Yes, maybe you should have.

MARGARET. But I didn't

(*to* **DOG**)

and do you know why? Because there was someone else to think about. Someone not so selfish

(pointing at **JAMES***)*

as this one!

JAMES. God only knows how she could have a frigid bitch like you for a mother.

MARGARET. April had a role model. Me! Someone who's *achieved*. And then there's you. No wonder she jumped all over the place, science-club, majorettes, Young Republicans, Peace Corps. It's amazing she wound up as good as she did.

JAMES. I helped.

MARGARET. Helped what? I was the one who stayed up with her as a baby. So colicky, always poor digestion that child. You always busy, busy with your gambling buddies –

JAMES. I helped. All her studying, who stayed up? With those multiplication cards? Who? And the history quizzes. That girl *loved* history, coming home with all those books. The Assyrians, Aztecs. No wonder she went with Anthropology. Peace Corps makes a lot of sense. That girl has *feelings*. Not like you.

MARGARET. I had feelings too … Until you killed them! With your Orange Julius! With your indolence! With your *ponies*! Always had to bet the fucking ponies, didn't you. Every Thursday …

JAMES. April, she wanted a pony once, remember?

MARGARET. Yes, but all we could afford back then. Thanks to you! Thanks to your little habit, was, what was it, a gerbil?

JAMES. Yes, a gerbil, I think so. Snickles, wasn't that his name?

MARGARET. Mr. Pickles!

(to **DOG**, *points to her head)*

See, not much left.

(to **JAMES***)*

It was Mr. Pickles! God did she love that little gerbil.

The way she'd cuddle ... and then when he had the accident.

JAMES. No accident! It was a stroke. What the vet said. Remember how he'd crawl around with just his two front legs.

(demonstrates)

And how she held him? All night long? Remember? ... Do you remember?

MARGARET. Yes, yes, I remember. The vet. It's best for, for Mr. Pickles, to be put down. Out of his misery? And we were worried. About April.

JAMES. But it was OK!

MARGARET. Yes, it was OK. After it was over. She was smiling. God, April loved that gerbil! Such compassion. "He's happy now." That's what she said. Five years old. "He's happy now!" Couldn't bear to see something in misery. Something she *loved*. That's how strong she felt!

DOG. *(pause, pointing to masks/animal carvings)* She got you those right?

MARGARET. Those things, yeah. She brought them home when she visited last month and put them up there. Funny looking.

(pause, to everyone)

So what are we going to do?

DOG. *(breaking tension)* Do?

MARGARET. About all this!

(waves arms around)

And about you. You were going to kill me right?

DOG. No, no, I was here just for silver. Just the silver.

MARGARET. To kill and steal from me. From me!

DOG. Silver. Just silver ...

MARGARET. *(to **JAMES**)* Maybe we can *use* him.

JAMES. *(excited)* Yeah?

MARGARET. The Bonnie and Clyde.

JAMES. I want the Bonnie.

MARGARET. *(to* **DOG** *)* You see? Always him first. Always OHH MOMMY! What does he care if I'm finished, if I'm … happy?

(pause)

No, I think it's time. Time for me. Time for …

JAMES. No, please.

MARGARET. Time for that … Yes, this is the time! Oh, yeah, baby!

JAMES. No, no, baby. You can't *make* him. I've got a gun too, remember baby?

MARGARET. Right, a role-play gun.

(to **DOG** *)*

You see, delusional!

(pause, while **DOG** *takes in that both identical guns are fakes and that* **JAMES** *and* **MARGARET** *both know that he knows.)*

(Slowly, **DOG** *rises. He moves to the table, picks up the tray which he had earlier chosen.)*

DOG. Man, you know, I don't know.

(inspects tray)

19th Century Flemish? Dunno.

(carefully inspecting tray)

Norstroms, did they have a branch in Antwerp. In the 19th century?

(returns tray, **MARGARET/JAMES** *start to react,* **DOG** *quickly moves to the door)*

No, no please. Listening. Listening skills, didn't your counselor tell you about listening. Shhh. Now this is important. I may not know much about silver. But these

(indicates masks)

these I know about. Take this one –

(removes largest mask from wall, a savage-looking face. At this point, his accent could begin to change to West African)

They say you know, my tribe, my *family*. Savages. Blood-thirsty cannibals.

(shrugs)

Ancient history! And wrong. Wrong! You know what I think. Craftsmen, *artists*, that's what we really are. Now look at this. Notice the even plasticity of form. And these lips. The blue highlights? You think that's *EASY*? Too much wassoomy leaf and it comes out purple – AND YET –

(softly)

and yet too much kookleberry juice, even a drop, and all you get is a crude red, almost a fuchsia! … Artists.

(Quickly, he removes a gun from behind the mask and shoots both JAMES and MARGARET. They fall on top of one another, JAMES' head in MARGARET's lap.)

(After a moment, DOG picks up the phone. He dials a lot of numbers.)

DOG. April? April, baby, it's over. No more suffering sweetheart. They're happy now … They're happy now.

(Curtain.)

TALL GRASS

CHARACTERS

CHESTER 80's
DOTTIE 80's, Chester's wife
HOWARD 20's-30's, a government worker

SETTING

A living room.

TIME

2007.

(Curtain opens on an elderly couple, **CHESTER** *and* **DOTTIE**, *seated in matching Barcolounger recliners. A cylindrical plant sits akimbo on a table. Next to* **DOTTIE**'s *chair rests a walker, with tennis balls over the front legs. She is asleep, snoring softly, with a long unfinished macramé tassel on her lap.* **CHESTER** *glances at the front door, checks his watch, glances at the front door again. A small bundle of mail drops through the slot in the front door. He pounces on it.)*

CHESTER. Thank you! Thank you!

(He opens a small brown package, revealing a cassette tape, and inserts it in an old portable player. Faintly at first, but then louder, we hear rap music. **CHESTER** *appears puzzled but then captures the rhythm. He dances a bit.* **DOTTIE** *opens her eyes and watches.)*

DOTTIE. Too old.

CHESTER. Huh?

DOTTIE. Old man! What do you think you're doing?

CHESTER. I'm playing music.

DOTTIE. What?

CHESTER. I'm playing music!

DOTTIE. What for?

CHESTER. For pleasure.

DOTTIE. Please turn that off.

*(***CHESTER** *turns off the music.)*

DOTTIE. You're no longer in your second childhood. You've graduated to your second adolescence.

CHESTER. I joined a club. A music club.

DOTTIE. A music club. At your age?

CHESTER. A new record is going to come every month.

DOTTIE. I don't want to hear it. Too violent.

CHESTER. Maybe we can get an iPod? They come with earphones.

DOTTIE. A what?

CHESTER. An iPod. It's like a Walkman except it hooks into computers.

DOTTIE. 82-year-old men do not use computers.

CHESTER. Well, how bout instead we get a –

DOTTIE. You are not getting a bicycle.

CHESTER. I want one!

DOTTIE. You can't drive a car, now you want to try a bicycle?

CHESTER. I can too drive a car. It's the driving *tests* I can't do … Clinton rides a bicycle.

DOTTIE. Bush.

CHESTER. Bush, no, he lost –

DOTTIE. The *new* Bush. The son. The one who likes war. He's the President now.

CHESTER. I could put a basket on. I could go to the plaza again. Bring stuff back for you.

DOTTIE. Let's do the mail.

(As **CHESTER** *sifts through the mail, an item catches his attention.*)

CHESTER. Dottie, look at this. We've won! A free trip. To Miami. We've been selected!

(**CHESTER** *hands over the envelope to* **DOTTIE** *who inspects it.*)

DOTTIE. We've been selected to enter a sweepstakes. Which costs $15. We haven't won anything Chester. It's a scam.

CHESTER. I've always wanted to visit Miami.

DOTTIE. You *have* visited Miami, back in '58. Remember when we stayed at the, you remember…the "theme" hotel.

CHESTER. The mirrors! That was Miami?

DOTTIE. Yes it was.

CHESTER. The mirrors. And the palm trees. Remember how I got? I thought I was going to shoot straight through you –

DOTTIE. Oh god.

CHESTER. Let's go to Miami. The mirrors, the palm trees –

DOTTIE. What you need is protein, not palm trees … And with my legs, the way they are.

CHESTER. I could help you …

DOTTIE. Oh Chester.

(**CHESTER** *goes to her and they embrace, share a brief kiss.* **CHESTER** *kisses* **DOTTIE** *again, starts to get a bit adventurous.*)

DOTTIE. That's enough.

(**DOTTIE** *begins sifting through the mail, tossing each into the garbage.*)

Catalog, another sweepstakes –

(**CHESTER** *briefly lights up.*)

– catalogue, the social security

(*tears in half and tosses with relish*)

Oh, look. Something from Maury.

CHESTER. Maury?

DOTTIE. Maury. Our son.

CHESTER. Our son's name is Maurice.

DOTTIE. Maury is the same thing as Maurice!

(*opening card*)

My goodness. Look how big they've gotten.

(*passes a photo to* **CHESTER**)

See. That's Lauren, Freddy and Charles.

(**CHESTER** *inspects the pictures.*)

Your grandchildren.

CHESTER. This one has a mustache.

DOTTIE. That's Charles, he was named after you.

CHESTER. My name is Chester.

DOTTIE. Ch, both of your names start with Ch.

CHESTER. So are they going to visit us?

(DOTTIE snorts.)

DOTTIE. *(reading)* "Bountiful love to my parents on Tank– ."

(squinting)

That boy always had the worst penmanship.

(hands card to CHESTER)

CHESTER. "Bountiful love to my parents on Thanksgiving."

(squints and moves card back and forth)

Dear folks, wishing you a terrific Thanksgiving. Hope you still recognize everyone. We're all doing fine here, but we worry a lot about you two. It's not healthy living all by yourselves like you do, way out in the house. So, we've done a little talking and found this place. It's called Happy Springs Village –

DOTTIE. No!

CHESTER. No what?

DOTTIE. No Happy Springs Village.

CHESTER. What's Happy Springs Village?

DOTTIE. That place he just mentioned. I think it's a nursing home.

CHESTER. *(continuing to read)* Now first off, I know what you're thinking. Happy Springs is not a nursing home. Happy Springs is a dynamic – dynamic, that's underlined in red by the way

(shows DOTTIE)

Happy Springs is a dynamic community of active – that's also underlined, active – seniors living independently but with all the services to make life easier. They have a wide variety of activities like shuffleboard –

DOTTIE. Shuffleboard? Why not baseball or soccer, basketball – what everyone else plays.

CHESTER. You want to play basketball?

DOTTIE. If forced to, I'd take basketball over shuffleboard yes … It's a nursing home Chester. They just don't call them that anymore. Everything's "Happy." It's all marketing.

CHESTER. *(continues reading)* … like shuffleboard, checkers, canasta, rummy, cribbage, bingo –

DOTTIE. Bingo!

CHESTER. I'm good at bingo.

DOTTIE. Checkers, but no chess? They think old people aren't smart enough to play chess.

CHESTER. *(continues reading)* Bingo and a wide variety of arts and crafts –

(points to **DOTTIE***'s tassel)*

That's a craft, you know.

(reading)

Residents also get to participate in daily music sing-alongs –

DOTTIE. Michael rowed the boat ashore, Haleluuu… Yah!! I'd rather die … You know what goes on in those places. Remember on 60 Minutes? Everything is regimented, you have to do arts and crafts whenever they tell you, have to eat whenever they tell you –

CHESTER. I bet they give you a lot of protein there.

DOTTIE. *(twisting and snapping the macramé)* You have no privacy in a place like that, no dignity, no independence. They have nurses, who come in and steal things and they just walk in without knocking. Even if you're naked …

*(***DOTTIE*** is weeping.)*

CHESTER. Dottie … Dottie … Don't worry Dottie.

DOTTIE. I want to stay here Chester.

CHESTER. Dottie, we're not going anywhere. This is our home.

DOTTIE. If we do go to Happy Rest or wherever, they're going to do everything for us. And pretty soon, you start relying on them. Then they're feeding you, bathing you, telling you what to do and when. Next thing you know you're helpless. Unable to do anything for yourself. Like a baby.

CHESTER. I won't let that happen.

DOTTIE. But eventually they come for you Chester. Remember on 60 Minutes?

CHESTER. No Dottie. 60 Minutes isn't always right. That's not going to happen to us.

DOTTIE. We're getting weaker Chester.

CHESTER. Look outside Dottie. The grass. See how tall the grass is?

DOTTIE. Yes, I know.

CHESTER. *(tosses card aside)* No Happy Rest!

(As **CHESTER** *and* **DOTTIE** *share another brief embrace, a soft knock is heard at the door.* **CHESTER** *and* **DOTTIE** *freeze. The knock repeats and* **CHESTER** *scrambles to the door revealing* **HOWARD***, a young man, dressed in a suit.)*

HOWARD. Hello, I'm from the government and I'm here to help.

(suddenly offering his hand)

*(***CHESTER** *recoils.)*

HOWARD. I can come back.

(starts to close door)

DOTTIE. *(struggling out of chair)* Chester!

*(***CHESTER** *reopens door.)*

HOWARD. I didn't mean to disturb you. Here.

(fumbling for business card).

Howard Farmington, Department of Health and Human Services. I'm new. Well not really new, myself. New to the department.

CHESTER. *(reading business card)* Junior Associate?

HOWARD. Junior Associate. Just for now. But if they like me, I can get an entry-level, a G-5. But that's like 50-50.

DOTTIE. Would you like to come in?

HOWARD. You're not busy?

CHESTER. We were just starting the mail.

DOTTIE. Chester!

(to **HOWARD***)*

This is Chester my husband. And I'm Dottie.

(offers her hand)

HOWARD. Very pleased to meet you. Howard Farmington –
Wow, that's quite some handshake!

DOTTIE. *(laughing)* My hands are the only things still working.

CHESTER. She does macramé.

(**DOTTIE** *twists the tassel between her hands, then snaps it.*)

HOWARD. I've been trying to call you for days. No one
answered so I thought I should drop by. I was really
worried when I saw how tall the grass is.

CHESTER. The grass is tall?

HOWARD. Yes very tall. Like it hasn't been mowed in months.
You really shouldn't let it get like that – people will
think that the house is abandoned or that you aren't
well enough to take care of it. There's a lot of preda-
tors out there, all sorts of unwelcome guests.

CHESTER. We like guests.

HOWARD. Well thanks … So, would you like to know why
I'm here?

DOTTIE. That would be nice.

HOWARD. Sure. Let me try to explain. I'm in sort of what
you would call the marketing department. The marketing department of the Elder Care Division.

CHESTER. Elder care? We don't need any care. And we're
not elders.

DOTTIE. Chester stop that. We are too elders. When are
you going to grow up? …

(to **HOWARD***)*

Please go on.

HOWARD. OK, well, you know the government. They've
got all kinds of services, right? And they've got a lot of
them in particular for you guys, for elders – for seniors,
like yourselves. But the only problem is, not everyone
seems to know about these services. There are thou-
sands, maybe millions, of seniors living out there, having
a hard time, but not even knowing about the kinds of

services available, helpful services, which can make their lives so much easier. That's what my job is, to make sure everyone that's eligible can get all the help they deserve. When I got your names and found out you live way out here by yourselves, I thought I could help you.

CHESTER. You got our names?

HOWARD. The government has everyone's names Mr. Madigan.

DOTTIE. We know that. We watch 60 Minutes ... So you'd like to help us?

HOWARD. Yes, absolutely. I'd love to help you. That is, if you qualify. We have to determine what needs you might have and then match the services to those needs.

CHESTER. That sounds complicated.

HOWARD. Well,

(pulls out a form)

This is the GRE822-I ... It's a survey, maybe more like a questionnaire. We'll need to fill this out.

CHESTER. A test? Is it like a test?

HOWARD. A test? No, not at all. All it does is determine what needs you may have. Once we know your needs we can then get to work finding the services to match those needs ... But we don't have to fill it out now. If you're not ready.

DOTTIE. Go ahead.

HOWARD. You sure?

DOTTIE. You didn't come all the way out here for nothing. Let's do it.

HOWARD. OK, well let's see. I haven't actually administered this test – the survey before. Some of the questions might be a little weird, OK? ... Right, the first question is, What year is it?

DOTTIE. What year is it? That's the question? Let me see. 1945. And I'm very busy now getting ready for the prom – What do you think we're senile?

HOWARD. No, no, I don't think that. I have to ask the questions or they won't pay me.

DOTTIE. 2007, and it's November 16th,

> *(checks clock)*

> 2:36 pm.

HOWARD. I don't write the questions. Really.

CHESTER. I knew that one too.

HOWARD. What?

CHESTER. I knew it was 2007.

HOWARD. Maybe we shouldn't do this right now.

DOTTIE. Next question!

HOWARD. You sure? OK. The next question is … Who is the President? –

CHESTER. Bush! The young feisty one … Right?

HOWARD. Yes, that's right. OK, we're done with that. We can move on to the next section now. Let's see, Medical. That last part was Mental by the way.

DOTTIE. We figured that.

HOWARD. OK, medical. Let me start with you Mrs. Madigan. How many medications do you take on a daily basis?

DOTTIE. *(points to medicine bottles on table)* I don't know, a couple of hundred.

HOWARD. Five, I count five.

> *(jotting down)*

> And you Mr. Madigan?

CHESTER. I'm on Anacin and One a Day Silver.

DOTTIE. One a Day is a vitamin, not a medicine!

HOWARD. And do you need any help with your medicines?

DOTTIE. *(twisting and snapping macramé)* What do you mean?

HOWARD. Help paying for them. Are you covered by Medicare?

DOTTIE. Medicare? Oh no, we don't believe in handouts.

HOWARD. Medicare is not a handout. It's just like Social Security. It's coming to you.

CHESTER. We don't do Social Security.

HOWARD. What? Everyone gets social security at your age.

DOTTIE. Look here young man. Don't go telling us what to do. We don't believe in *handouts*, get it? Not from the government, not from our son, not from Happy Times Rest Home. Not from anything or anybody. We're not going to end up like my mother, helpless, like a baby. We're not going to get started down that road, the road to *dependency*. We're independent, *self-sufficient.*

(points to plant)

Like that plant. Water and sunlight is all it needs.

CHESTER. And flies! ... That's not a regular plant. It's a pitcher plant. Catches flies.

HOWARD. I didn't mean to offend you.

DOTTIE. You haven't offended us. I just wanted to make a point.

HOWARD. Please accept my –

DOTTIE. It's OK.

HOWARD. *(jotting)* All right then, so not covered by Medicare. Let's go to transportation. What is your primary mode of transportation?

DOTTIE. Transportation? With these legs?

CHESTER. Her legs are weak, but mine are strong! I used to play soccer you know. In college.

(demonstrates with surprising agility)

DOTTIE. Chester has the body of a 60-year-old man. That's what the doctor said. Even though he's 82. He's amazing. The only problem is he thinks he has the body of an 18-year-old.

HOWARD. That's good to know. May I ask if you still drive?

CHESTER. No. They just took my license away.

DOTTIE. Not "just." 8 years ago. 8 years ago this Tuesday we lost the license.

HOWARD. I know how you feel. I also lost a license.

CHESTER. You don't drive either?

HOWARD. A different kind of license. But I like this job better. It allows me to help people... . So do you have someone who drives you?

DOTTIE. Drives us? No.

HOWARD. What if you need to go somewhere? … You know, like shopping.

DOTTIE. Oh, we don't shop. That's for young people.

HOWARD. You don't shop?

CHESTER. Maybe if I had a bicycle, I could make it to the plaza.

DOTTIE. Stop with the bicycle!

(*to* **HOWARD**)

See what I mean?

(*back to* **CHESTER**)

You think you're 18 years old? What happens when you fall off the bicycle? And break your hip. Two of us like this. Then what are we going to do?

HOWARD. How about a taxi?

DOTTIE. A taxi? Dear, not even Dominos comes way out here.

HOWARD. Well then, how do you get your medicines?

(*points to medicines*)

DOTTIE. In the mail.

HOWARD. (*jotting down*) Shut-ins.

DOTTIE. What was that?

HOWARD. You're shut-ins. You know, people who never leave the house.

DOTTIE. No, we're not shut ins. We leave the house all the time. Just this morning Chester went out to check on the sprinklers.

HOWARD. I don't mean just around the yard.

DOTTIE. Young man, haven't you been listening? We lost the license 8 years ago. Where can we possibly go? … Don't look so surprised. You think old people can't learn new things? But we can. We adapt.

HOWARD. I hope I can be as independent as you two when I get to be your age.

DOTTIE. Thank you …

HOWARD. OK, well, we're almost done here. Transportation ... Let's see. What's next? Security. Do you have a home security system installed?

CHESTER. What do we need that for?

HOWARD. Mr. Madigan, that's not good. Not good at all.

Do you realize older people are 10.9 times more likely to be a victim of a crime than the rest of the population? And you two, living all by yourselves and with the grass so tall – it's like an open invitation ... Hasn't anyone ever tried to rob you?

CHESTER. Oh, sure, they try.

DOTTIE. But not for a long while.

HOWARD. Well next time you might not be so lucky. We'll have to order you one.

DOTTIE. The government is going to make us get a home security system?

HOWARD. The government has to ensure that all of its citizens are properly protected ... There's one thing though. It's going to take a little while to order the security system. It might not arrive for a couple of weeks. You're going to need some protection before that.

DOTTIE. You sure worry a lot for someone your age.

HOWARD. Worrying is my job. You don't want someone to break in and steal all your valuables do you? ... Your jewelry, your clothes, your appliances, your TV, your identities –

DOTTIE. They can steal our identities?

CHESTER. I saw a movie on that. Zontar and the Pod People –

HOWARD. It's very easy to steal someone's identity. All they need is to get a hold of one of your credit card receipts. Do you have any of those around the house?

DOTTIE. Credit cards? No. That's a form of debt.

HOWARD. How about a bank account statement then. You have a checking account right?

DOTTIE. Yes, of course.

HOWARD. May I see it? … Your checking account statement. I want to make sure it's OK.

DOTTIE. You'd like to see our bank statement?

HOWARD. It's for your own benefit. I'm trying to help you.

DOTTIE. Maybe in there.

(*points to the mail pile*)

(**HOWARD** *retrieves a statement and reads it. He whistles.*)

DOTTIE. We've been careful. Not like my mother was.

HOWARD. $250,000. Earning no interest. The bank is taking advantage of you and that gets me angry.

CHESTER. You sure know a lot about money.

HOWARD. I didn't always work for the government.

(*pockets the bank statement*)

Now, it's very important that we keep everything safe until the security system is installed…. Do you have anything else? Any other valuables around here? Jewelry?

DOTTIE. My jewelry?

HOWARD. We don't want that stolen. The government will take care of it for you.

DOTTIE. You want to take my jewelry?

HOWARD. Not take. Safeguard. And just for a little while. A couple of days. Maybe less. Then we'll give it right back to you.

DOTTIE. I never heard of the government keeping people's jewelry.

CHESTER. What if she doesn't want to give it to you?

HOWARD. Mr. and Mrs. Madigan, do you understand I'm trying to help you? The government can't afford to have its citizens in such risk. It's for your own benefit. Two people of your age, living way out here by yourself, it's not safe. We can't allow you to go on like this. I'd really like to keep you living in your own house … if possible …

CHESTER. 60 Minutes was right.

HOWARD. Mrs. Madigan, please let me help you. Don't

make this more difficult than it has to be…

DOTTIE. Chester, I think this young man is trying to help us. Do you think we should give him the box? … Chester? The box?

CHESTER. The box? OK.

HOWARD. What box are you talking about?

DOTTIE. The box. The lockbox. Where we keep the jewelry. All our important things. The rest of the money … We don't want to keep too much in the bank.

HOWARD. A lockbox? Yes, of course. We're going to have to keep that safe.

(**DOTTIE** *reaches under her chair and slowly pulls out a large metal box. In the process, she wrenches her shoulder.*)

HOWARD. Let me help you.

(**HOWARD** *bends down to reach for the box, but* **DOTTIE** *nudges it further under the chair. As* **HOWARD** *reaches for the box,* **CHESTER** *savagely kicks him.* **HOWARD** *loses his footing.* **DOTTIE** *swiftly wraps the macramé cord around his neck.* **HOWARD** *struggles upwards, but is kicked again by* **CHESTER**. *He lurches, grappling with* **DOTTIE**, *but she does not release her grip.* **CHESTER** *kicks him again, and again.* **HOWARD**, *reaches for* **DOTTIE**, *then stops. He spasms a bit and is still.*)

(*After a moment,* **DOTTIE** *removes the tassel from around* **HOWARD**'s *neck. She flexes her wrists and snaps the macramé. She rearranges* **HOWARD**'s *tie, fixes his hair. She gently kisses his forehead.*)

CHESTER. He was nice.

DOTTIE. Yes. He's going to be a great help to us.

(*opens the lockbox and removes a huge axe*)

Full of protein. Not stringy like the last two.

(*Rap music comes on as lights fade to red.*)

(*Curtain.*)

PROP LIST

Prop#	Qty.	Prop	Character	Pt-Sc-Pg	Preset/Location	Notes
1.1	1	Backstage Chair A	furniture	1-1-01		for backstage, paint black
1.2	1	Backstage Chair B	furniture	1-1-01		for backstage, paint black
5	1	Centerpiece, small	dressing	1-1-01	OS: table A	w/ grass
6	1	Candle	dressing	1-1-01	OS: table A	lit, possibly preset lit, one tealight per show?
7	2	Dinner Plates w/ remains of meal	Waiter/Paula/Trevor	1-1-01	OS: table A	
9	2	Forks	Waiter/Paula/Trevor	1-1-01	OS: table A	
10	2	Knives	Waiter/Paula/Trevor	1-1-01	OS: table A	
11	2	Napkins	Waiter/Paula/Trevor	1-1-01	OS: table A	cloth
12	1	Blackberry	Paula	1-1-03	OS: table A: purse	thrown against wall on 1/3/27, hear it buzz (sound C
13	1	Purse	Paula	1-1-03*	OS: table A: purse	costume
14	2	Trays	Waiter	1-1-05	DR prop table	
15	1	Ring Box	Trevor	1-1-06	DR prop table	do we need to see the ring?
16	1	Coffee Cup & Saucer	Waiter	1-1-06	DR prop table: tray 1	no liquid needed - not drunk
17	1	Espresso Cup & Saucer	Waiter	1-1-06	DR prop table: tray 1	no liquid needed - not drunk
18	1	Champagne Bottle	Waiter	1-1-11	DR: ice bucket	not opened/poured
19		Champagne/Ginger Ale		1-3-25	DR prop table	2 glasses/show
20.1	1	Champagne flutes	Waiter/Paula/Trevor	1-3-25	UR prop table	
20.2	1	Champagne flutes	Waiter/Paula/Trevor	1-1-06	DR prop table	
21	1	Flatscreen Computer Monitor	Paula	1-2-12	SL: table B	
22	1	Computer Keyboard	dressing	1-2-12	SL: table B	
23	1	Office Phone, multi-line	Paula	1-2-12	UL: file box	
26	1	Coffee mug	Paula	1-2-12	UR prop table	
30	1	Letter of Resignation	Trevor	1-2-18	DR prop table	Trevor hands it to Paula, bears his signature
31	2	Menus	Waiter/Paula/Trevor	1-3-25	UL prop table	refer to "specials" on the menu
32	1	Trevor's Gun	Trevor	1-3-38	DR prop table	fire blanks? Sound effect? Not fired?
33	1	Waiter's Gun	Waiter	1-3-38	DR prop table	fire blanks? Sound effect? Shoots Trevor
34	2	Steak Knife	Paula	1-3-38	UL prop table	used to stab Waiter, blood knife?
36	1	Cabinet	set	2-1-01*	OS	scenic element - part of wall
37	1	Fine China	dressing	2-1-01	OS: cabinet	
38	1	Silver	dressing	2-1-01	OS: cabinet	
39	1	Cabinet Decorations	dressing	2-1-01	OS: cabinet	TBD - depending what we need to dress cabinet
40		Family Photos	dressing	2-1-01	OS: cabinet top	including one that looks like April, the daughter
41	2+	African Masks	dressing/Dog	2-1-01	OS: cabinet top	more than one - referred to as "those", one hides gu
43	1	Ice Cream Container	James	2-1-01	DR prop table	
44		Ice cream	James	2-1-01	DR prop table	would like to see him eat real ice cream, if possible
45	1	Spoon	James	2-1-01	DR prop table	
46	1	Carving Knife	James	2-1-01	OS: cabinet: bottom	wielded, not used in combat
47	1	Cordless Phone		2-1-01		
48	1	Larger Knife	Dog	2-1-01	OS: cabinet: bottom	wielded, not used in combat
49	1	James' Gun	James	2-1-01	DR prop table	not fired
50	1	Silver Tray		2-1-07	OS: cabinet	Flemish
51	1	Silver piece TBA		2-1-09	OS: cabinet	Rococo
52	2	Silver Goblet		2-1-09	OS: cabinet	NOT matching
53	1	Margaret's Gun	Margaret	2-1-14	UL prop table	not fired
54	1	Dog's Gun	Dog	2-1-22	OS: cabinet: behind mask	fired 2x (sound effect?)
55	1	Pitcher Plant	dressing	3-1-01		ref. by Howard, Chester describes it as pitcher plant
56	1	Walker w/ Tennis Balls	Dottie	3-1-01		
57	1	knitting (circular needles)	Dottie	3-1-01		

PROP LIST

#	Qty.	Prop	Character	Pt-Sc-Pg	Preset/Location	Notes
58	*1*	*Watch*	*Chester*	3-1-01		*costume?*
59	1	Bundle of Mail	Chester	3-1-01	DR prop table	mail, catalogues, sweepstake-like envelopes
60	1	Brown Package	Chester	3-1-01	DR: in mail bundle	opened each night - probably can re-seal & reuse
61	1	Cassette Tape	Chester	3-1-01	DR: in brown package	put into cassette player, practical?
62	1	Portable Cassette Player	Chester	3-1-01		cassette tape inserted into player, practical?
63	1/sh	Sweepstakes Envelope	Chester/Dottie	3-1-03	DR: in mail bundle	opened by Dottie
64	1	Sweepstakes Letter	Chester/Dottie	3-1-03	DR: in sweeps envelope	
65	1/sh	Maury Envelope		3-1-05	DR: in mail bundle	opened each night
66	1	Thanksgiving Card		3-1-05	DR: in Maury envelope	
67	1	Maury Photo		3-1-05	DR: in card	photo of Maury's 3 kids
68	1	Business Card	Howard	3-1-08	DR prop table	
69	1/sh	Form GRE 822-I	Howard	3-1-08	DR prop table	survey form, Howard fills it out
70	5	Medication Bottles		3-1-15		Howard counts 5 bottles on table
71	1	Bank Statement		3-1-18	DR: in mail bundle	
72	1	Lockbox		3-1-19		
73	1	Huge Axe		3-1-20		
74	1	knitted Plant Holder	Dressing	3-1-01		
75	TBD	Old Mail/Newspapers	Dressing	3-1-01		
77	2	Wine Glasses	Paula/Trevor/Waiter	1-1-01	OS: table A	with some liquid in them
79	1	Centerpiece, larger	dressing	2-1-01		
80	1	large stack of mail/newspapers	dressing	3-1-01		
81	1	sugar holder w/packets	Waiter	1-1-06	DR: tray	not used
82	1	creamer	Waiter	1-1-06	DR: tray	empty, not used
83	2	coffee spoons	Waiter	1-1-06	DR: tray	not used
84	1	Notepad	Paula	1-2-12	UL: file box	
85	1	Pen	Paula	1-2-12	UL: file box	also in 2-1-01 (on table)
87	1	"red wine"	Trevor/Paula	1-1-01	table A: in bottle	
88	1	Portfolio Folder w/ clipboard	Howard	3-1-08		w/ pocket inside cover for papers
89	1	TV	set	3-1-01	SL storage	old, gutted for lights
90	1	Newspaper	dressing	2-1-01		on table
91	1	silverware display box		2-1-01*	OS: cabinet: bottom	
92	1	silverware, various		2-1-01*	cabinet: in box	nice silver, includes other knives (46 and 48)
93	2	charger plates	dressing	1-3-25	DL prop table	
94	4	blanks				
95	1	briefcase, Paula's	Paula	1-2-12	UL: file box	
96	1	file box w/ lid	Paula	1-2-12	UL	has "La Brek, 4N" written on it
97	12	file folders	Paula/dressing	1-2-12	UL: file box 2: Paula's briefcase	
98	1	small tape measure	Paula	1-2-12	UL: file box	
99	5	government pamphlets	Howard	3-1-08	DR prop table	
100	2	clicky pens	Howard	3-1-08	DR prop table	
101	1/sh	social security check in envelope	Dottie	3-1-4*	DR prop table	torn in half onstage
102	1	trashcan	dressing/Dottie/Chester	3-1-01	UL prop table	overflowing with old mail, etc.
103	1	broom	Dottie	3-1-01	UL	
104	1	knitting basket w/ yarn, etc.	Dottie	3-1-01	UL	
105	1	binder w/ colored dividers	Paula	1-2-12	UR: Paula's bag	
106	1	camping chair	Dottie/sofa	1-3-25		to provide back support for Dottie on couch
107	1	ice bucket on stand	Paula/dressing	1-3-25	DR prop table	
108	1/sh	blood pack	Paula, etc.	1-3-38	OS: table A	
109	sev	towels	Waiter/Crew	1-3-40	UL prop table: bus tub	waiter's towels; used to clean blood

TALL GRASS

PROP LIST

Prop#	Qty.	Prop	Character	Pt-Sc-Pg	Preset/Location	Notes
110	1	small ziploc bag	Paula	1-2-15	UL: file box:shoe	
111	2	cigarettes	Paula	1-2-15	UL:file box:ziploc:shoe	not smoked
112	1 pr	old sneakers	Paula	1-2-15	UL:file box	not worn
113	1	pack of mini donuts	Paula	1-2-15	UL:paula's bag: brown bag	not eaten
114	1	paper bag	Paula	1-2-12	UR: Paula's bag	
114	1	lighter	Waiter		UL prop table	the long kind
115	1	neck pillow	Dottie	1-3-25	UR prop table	
1.3	1	Backstage Chair C	furniture	1-1-01		for backstage, paint black

COSTUME PLOT

Scene	TOD	Bottom	Shoes	Hair	Accessory	Underdress
1.1 Paula	blouse	tights black skirt	black pumps		dutch purse jewelry	camisole
CHANGE	Add jacket				remove purse add briefcase	
1.2	blouse jacket	tights black skirt	black pumps		briefcase jewelry	camisole
CHANGE	remove jacket remove blouse				rmv briefcase add purse	
1.3	camisole	tights black skirt	black pumps		dutch purse	
CHANGE	rmv camisole add nightgown add robe?	remove tights remove skirt	remove pumps add mules		remove all	
2.1 Margaret	nightgown robe?		mules			
-CHANGE	rmv robe? rmv nightgown	QofJ iQtf SKtfl	rmv mules add socks add shoes	add wig	add glasses addjewelry	
3.1 Dottie	green blouse daisy sweater	tan print skirt	tan shoes socks	wig	glasses jewelry	

COSTUME PLOT

Scene	Top	Bottom	Shoes	Hair	Accessory	Underdress
1.1 Trevor	striped shirt sport coat blue tie	navy pants	black socks oxblood shoes			
CHANGE	remove jacket remove tie add sweater vst					
1.2	striped shirt sweater vest	navy pants	black socks oxblood shoes			
CHANGE	rmv sweater vst add tie add jacket					
1.3	striped shirt suit jacket black tie	navy pants	black socks oxblood shoes	.		
CHANGE	remove jacket remove tie	remove pants add	remove shoes	stick back	add glasses	
2.1 James	red/grey robe	grey P.J bottoms	slippers	slicked back	glasses	
CHANGE	remove robe add shirt add tie add jacket	remove PJs add pants	remove slippers add socks add shoes	?	remove glasses (pin on jacket) (ID on jacket)	
3.1 Howard	cream shirt rust tie blue suit jacket	blue suit pants	black socks oxblood shoes	?	lapel pin ID badge clip	

COSTUME PLOT

ene	TOD	Bottom	Shoes	Hair	Accessory	Underdress
1-1.3 aiter	white shirt black vest tie	black pants waiter apron	black socks black shoes			undershirt?
HANGE	remove vest remove tie remove shirt add blacktop	remove apron	remove shoes change socks restore shoes		add mask	
2.1 b Jack top og		black pants	white socks black shoes		ninja mask	undershirt?
HANGE	remove top add button-down	remove pants add pants/susp	remove shoes add shoes	add hat	add watch	
3.1 undershirt hester	'button-down	wool pants suspenders	white socks brown shoes	tan hat	watch	

From the Reviews of
TALL GRASS...

"Farce is Brian Harris' métier – it allows the brutality of each relationship to creep up on you, heightening the dramatic tension in a way that Neil LaBute's handling of similar themes cannot."
- *The New York Times*

"Juicy, Entertaining and Dangerous! A woman becomes her boyfriend's boss, a man catches a burglar in his home, a con artist tries to dupe an elderly couple – each play veers towards violence and dark humor. The fizzy energy of a romantic comedy... a threatening sexual vibe!"
- *Variety*

"Unpredictable Tall Tales! Three surreal notions of the things we do for love."
- *The Village Voice*

"The dark, brutal underbelly of humanity is present in each character, perhaps making for a devastating look at modern life. Brian Harris' dialogue is fast, full of life, and showing these characters in all their complexities in such a short amount of time."
– *Edge Publications*

MAURITIUS
Theresa Rebeck

Comedy / 3m, 2f / Interior

Stamp collecting is far more risky than you think. After their mother's death, two estranged half-sisters discover a book of rare stamps that may include the crown jewel for collectors. One sister tries to collect on the windfall, while the other resists for sentimental reasons. In this gripping tale, a seemingly simple sale becomes dangerous when three seedy, high-stakes collectors enter the sisters' world, willing to do anything to claim the rare find as their own.

"(Theresa Rebeck's) belated Broadway bow, the only original play by a woman to have its debut on Broadway this fall."
- Robert Simonson, *New York Times*

"*Mauritius* caters efficiently to a hunger that Broadway hasn't been gratifying in recent years. That's the corkscrew-twist drama of suspense… she has strewn her script with a multitude of mysteries."
- Ben Brantley, *New York Times*

"Theresa Rebeck is a slick playwright… Her scenes have a crisp shape, her dialogue pops, her characters swagger through an array of showy emotion, and she knows how to give a plot a cunning twist."
- John Lahr, *The New Yorker*

EURYDICE
Sarah Ruhl

Dramatic Comedy / 5m, 2f / Unit Set

In *Eurydice*, Sarah Ruhl reimagines the classic myth of Orpheus through the eyes of its heroine. Dying too young on her wedding day, Eurydice must journey to the underworld, where she reunites with her father and struggles to remember her lost love. With contemporary characters, ingenious plot twists, and breathtaking visual effects, the play is a fresh look at a timeless love story.

"RHAPSODICALLY BEAUTIFUL. A weird and wonderful new play - an inexpressibly moving theatrical fable about love, loss and the pleasures and pains of memory."
- The New York Times

"EXHILARATING!! A luminous retelling of the Orpheus myth, lush and limpid as a dream where both author and audience swim in the magical, sometimes menacing, and always thrilling flow of the unconscious."
- *The New Yorker*

"Exquisitely staged by Les Waters and an inventive design team… Ruhl's wild flights of imagination, some deeply affecting passages and beautiful imagery provide transporting pleasures. They conspire to create original, at times breathtaking, stage pictures."
- *Variety*

"Touching, inventive, invigoratingly compact and luminously liquid in its rhythms and design, *Eurydice* reframes the ancient myth of ill-fated love to focus not on the bereaved musician but on his dead bride – and on her struggle with love beyond the grave as both wife and daughter."
- *The San Francisco Chronicle*

EVIL DEAD: THE MUSICAL
Book & Lyrics By George Reinblatt
Music By Frank Cipolla/Christopher Bond/Melissa Morris/ George Reinblatt

Musical Comedy / 6m, 4f / Unit set

Based on Sam Raimi's 80s cult classic films, *Evil Dead* tells the tale of 5 college kids who travel to a cabin in the woods and accidentally unleash an evil force. And although it may sound like a horror, its not! The songs are hilariously campy and the show is bursting with more farce than a Monty Python skit. *Evil Dead: The Musical* unearths the old familiar story: boy and friends take a weekend getaway at abandoned cabin, boy expects to get lucky, boy unleashes ancient evil spirit, friends turn into Candarian Demons, boy fights until dawn to survive. As musical mayhem descends upon this sleepover in the woods, "camp" takes on a whole new meaning with up-roarious numbers like "All the Men in my Life Keep Getting Killed by Candarian Demons," "Look Who's Evil Now" and "Do the Necronomicon."

Outer Critics Circle nomination for
Outstanding New Off-Broadway Musical

"The next Rocky Horror Show!"
- New York Times

"A ridiculous amount of fun."
- Variety

"Wickedly campy good time."
- Associated Press